Ebb and Flo
and their New Friend

Jane Simmons

ORCHARD BOOKS

To Neil,

who made it all possible

ORCHARD BOOKS
96 Leonard Street, London EC2A 4XD
Orchard Books Australia
32/45-51 Huntley Street, Alexandria, NSW 2015
ISBN 1 84362 842 2
First published in Great Britain in 1998
First paperback edition published in 1999
This edition published in 2005
Text and illustrations © Jane Simmons 1998
The right of Jane Simmons to be identified as the author and illustrator of this work has been
asserted by her in accordance with the Copyrights, Designs and Patents Act, 1988.
A CIP catalogue record for this book is available from the British Library.
1 3 5 7 9 10 8 6 4 2
Printed in Singapore

Ebb sat in her favourite spot.
Things couldn't be better.
Suddenly she heard a flapping noise . . .

. . . and there it sat, a bird, in Ebb's favourite spot.

Flo giggled.

"Beep, beep, beep," said the bird.

"Isn't she lovely, Ebb," said Flo. "You must share with her. She wants to be friends with you."

Ebb growled.

"Beep, beep, beep," said the bird.

That night Ebb did not sleep well.

As the days passed, Ebb got grumpier.
  "Look at that bird! Isn't she sweet?"
people would say.
  "Beep, beep, beep," said the bird.
  "Grrr, grrr," Ebb growled.

Even Granny liked Bird and fed it Ebb's titbits.
    "Beep, beep, beep," said the bird.
    Ebb wished Bird would fly far away
and never come back.

The very next morning, Ebb's wish came true.
"Oh no. Bird has gone!" cried Flo.

And when they went out, Ebb had her favourite spot all to herself. Things couldn't be better.

Only, she had to eat her dinner all by herself. It felt strange without Bird getting in the way.

And somehow she couldn't sleep very well now that she was alone. It was too quiet without Bird's beeping and her bed was too cold and empty.

Even at Granny's all she could think of was Bird. She didn't want her titbits. Ebb wasn't happy at all.

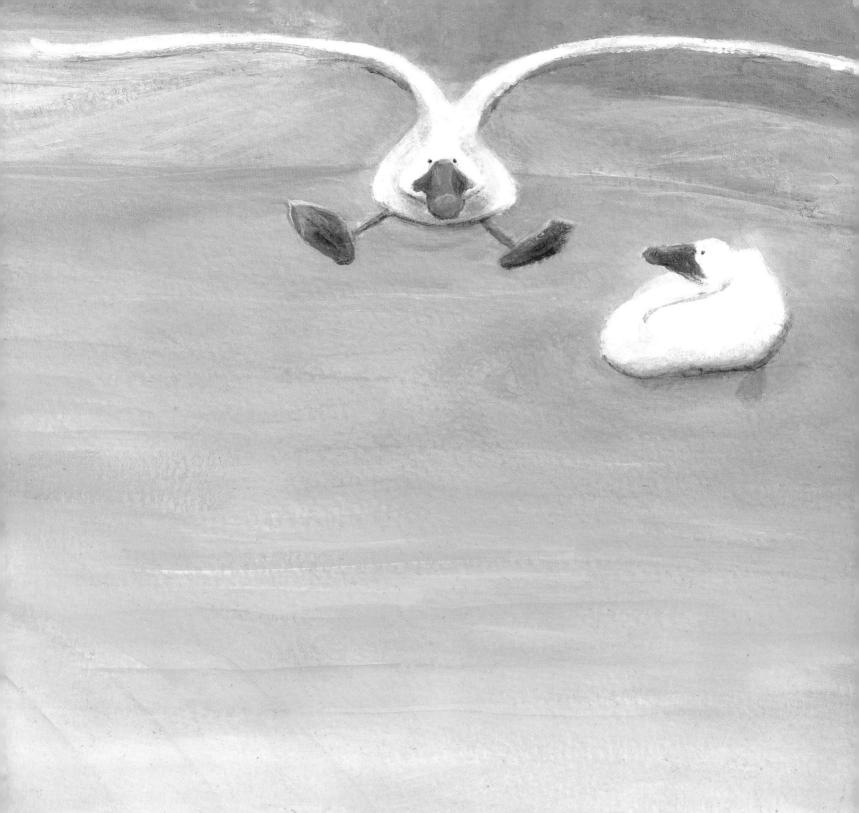

As the long hot summer days passed,
the dragonflies buzzed and the birds sang.
Ebb saw some geese on the river . . .

. . . but none of them swam
near the boat.

"Come on, Ebb," said Flo.
"Let's go fishing."

But it was no good. Ebb
missed Bird more than ever.

Then one day "Beep, beep, beep!" heard Ebb.
"Bird!" called Flo.
Ebb barked excitedly.

And there Bird sat in Ebb and
Bird's favourite spot . . .

Things couldn't be better.